# JOSEPHINE AND THE QUARANTINE

## QUARANTINE

By Candace Echols
Illustrated by Dare Harcourt

WestBow Press books may be ordered through booksellers or by contacting:

WestBow Press
A Division of Thomas Nelson & Zondervan
1663 Liberty Drive
Bloomington, IN 47403
www.westbowpress.com
844-714-3454

ISBN: 978-1-6642-0853-7 (sc)
ISBN: 978-1-6642-0852-0 (hc)
ISBN: 978-1-6642-0854-4 (e)

Library of Congress Control Number: 2020920069

Printed in the United States of America.

WestBow Press rev. date: 11-05-2020

To my dear Jim
and to Wrigley
-C.E.

To my incredible family
Pat, Craig, Kate Taylor,
Cam, and baby Liam Hart
-D.H.

And of course to our own little gifts
from Heaven... our pups
🩶 Rookie and Finn 🩶

Rookie Echols

Finn Harcourt

A dog was the friend that
Josephine needed.

She got on her knees.
She begged and she pleaded.

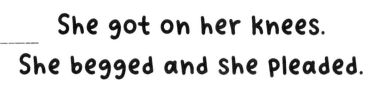

She cleaned up the yard.
She swept and she weeded.

But the answer was always the same:

"NO."

"But Mama," she said,
"I'm a dog-lover!
Whatever the cost,
I'll be happy to cover.
I promise I'll share him
with my little brother!"

"Dogs shed," was the answer that came.

"NO."

"In my heart, Mama, I own a puppy - not a cat, not a bird, not a horse or a guppy. I'll gladly trade in my lovie and buppy!"

"They're hyper
and tricky to
tame.

No."

The kind little girl was sad and frustrated.
She tried to be patient. She waited and waited.
"Should I ask again?" in her mind, she debated.

"Josephine, something has changed."

Whoa!

"A virus has spread
and now it's worldwide.
Some are just sick,
but others have died."

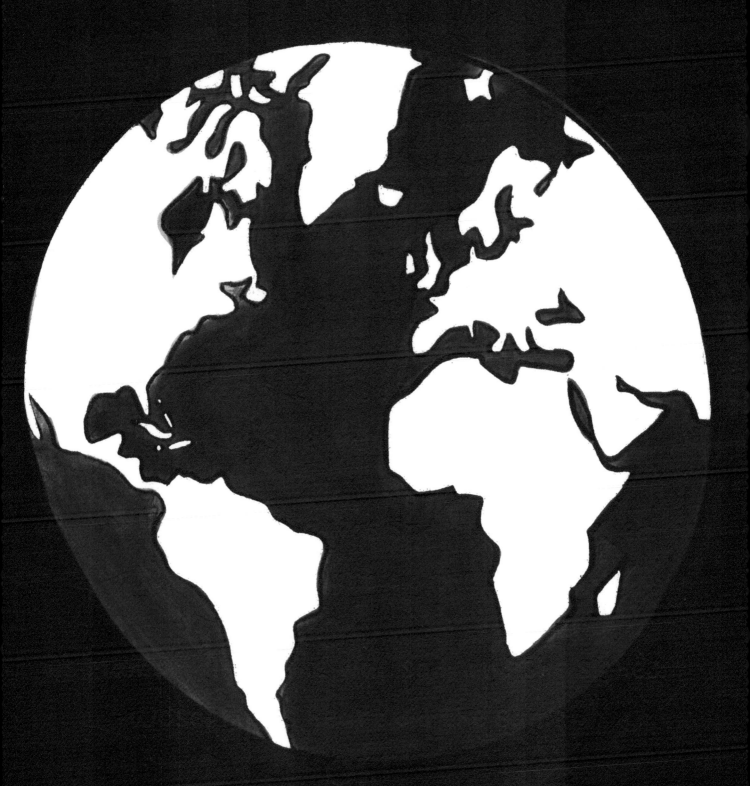

As Mama talked, she was sad, and she sighed.
Josephine's heart did the same.

Oh!

"But early today,
I went out for a run.
I saw zillions of families
having oodles of fun.
I considered the reasons,
and there was just one:

Dog adoptions had been arranged."

"I know!"

"The Jacksons showed me their pooch's new collar.

The Brown's dog is smart, so they call him 'Scholar.'

The Smith's pup is quick, and he's a real baller." Something in Mama's heart changed.

"And so?"

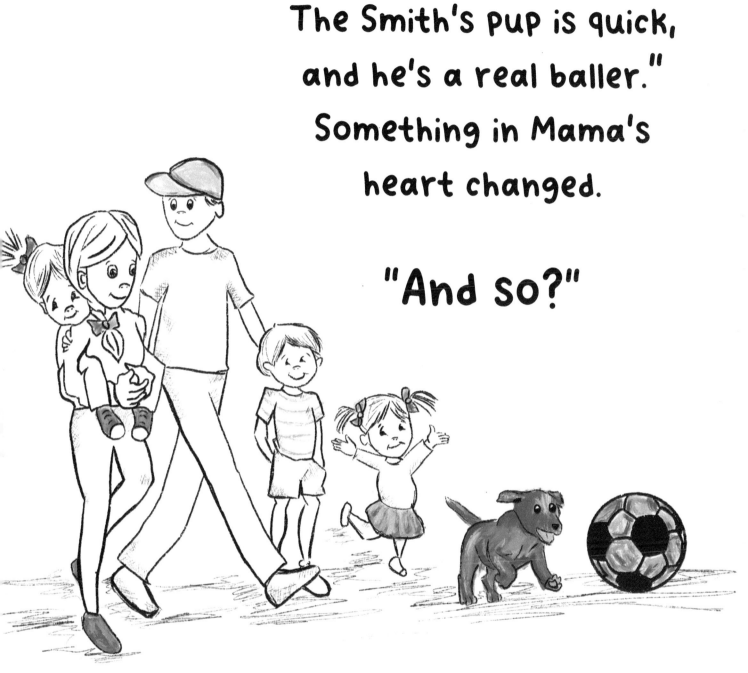

Quarantine makes
us all feel alone.
But God is still here,
and he hears
every groan.

He wants you to see
you are loved,
you are known.
That is the reason
He came.
Whoa!

"I've seen this miracle all over town:
Smiles have replaced some tears
and some frowns.
God shows his love through
the puppies around.

I think you and I are the same."

"Oh?"

"We feel God's love when we play with a dog....

They are with us to
comfort, protect, and to jog.
They stay by our side
in sunshine or fog.
They're like cuddles
from God every day!"

"And so?!"

"Let's get a dog to remind
us what's true:
Our Father cares for us
when we are blue.
Dogs are God's gifts
for me and for you!
Now all we need is a name..."


"Bo!"

"Every good and perfect gift is from above, coming down from the Father of the heavenly lights, who does not change like shifting shadows."
James 1:17

## Questions For Fun:

1. What do you notice about the illustrations in this book? Pay special attention to the front and back covers.

2. What do you think color stands for in this story?

3. What happens to Josephine's family as God's love fills their hearts?

4. How does God comfort you through His good creation?